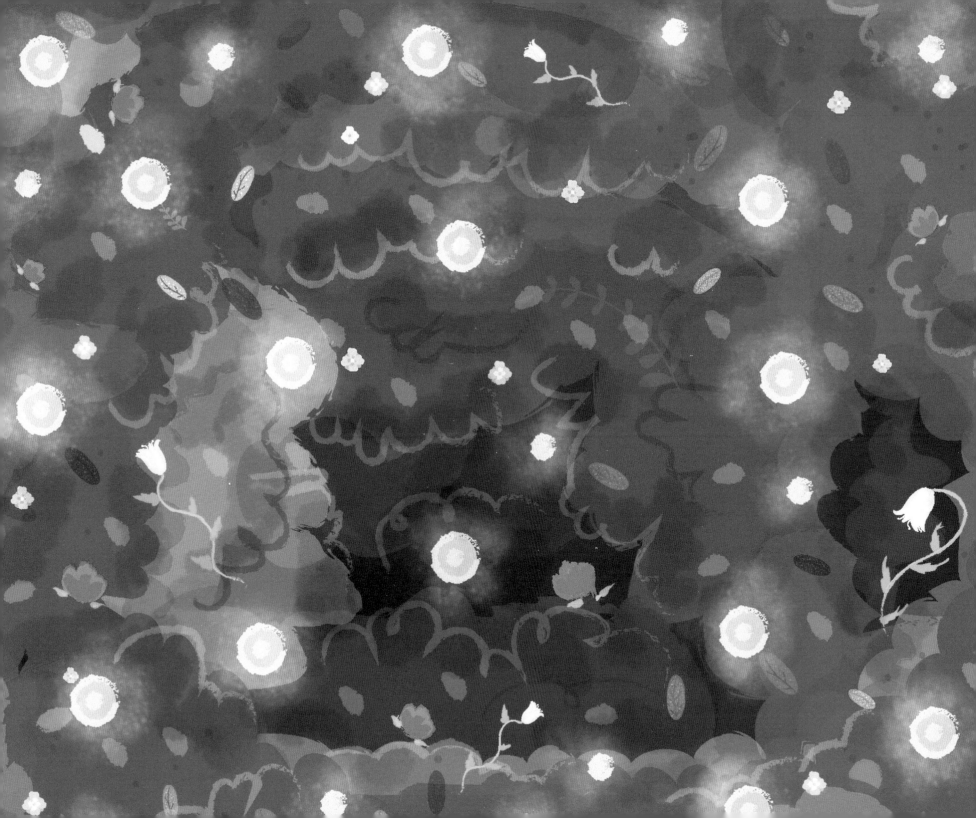

Fin the Fox

First Printing, 2018

ISBN 978-1-7330772-0-0

Fox Cottage Press LLC
New York, USA

Deep in the woods of
WayWayYonder,

Lived **a small fox named Fin,** who would often wonder.

He loved to gaze upon the fireflies' evening flights,

who illuminated the woods with their dazzling lights.

Their gift to the woods was enchanting glee,

as they nestled in the tall, glimmering trees.

Fin was a sweet and shy little fox.

He kept to himself and played his guitar.

Fin would fill the woods with his sweet songs,

as the fireflies happily danced along.

One night,

Fin curled up underneath a starry sky.

The fireflies nestled in the trees nearby as

he strummed on his guitar a sweet lullaby.

But little did they know...

Just way over yonder, A large hungry cloud was

making its way over to **Way Way Yonder.**

"These little lights look so yummy!"
The large cloud said as he floated through a brightly lit sky.

He was so hungry,
he opened his mouth.
One by one the fireflies
were gobbled up!

Fin woke up.

He watched as the fireflies
suddenly whirled by and the
night began to darken.

The animals of the woods knew something was wrong.

They shrieked, and they howled and some even hissed.

"**The moon has gone to sleep,**" the frogs began to croak.

"**Nonsense,**" scoffed the birds.

"**This is a serious matter, no place for a frog's jokes!**"

"**Excuse me,**" muttered Fin.

"**Not now little fox!**" they all yelled in unison.

Fin felt the joy leave the woods.

"Have any of you seen where the fireflies went?"

he quietly asked the animals by the river.

"Not a clue," each animal would say as they pushed by.

Fin was worried.

But he felt so small.

What could a small fox possibly do?

"I'll see what I can do, I guess,

Fin said aloud.

"I may be small,

but I'll give it my best."

Fin heard a voice and looked at some falling leaves.

" Hellooo! "

A little firefly
fluttered above his head.

"I have lost my family," she sadly said.

"Maybe you can come with me" Fin said

kindly. "We can search the woods together."

Together they crossed fields and streams.
Fin searched under every rock, and around every tree.
"A firefly!!" a small bear yelled and tumbled out of a nearby bush.

The small bear giggled and roared.

"I'm so big and brave, can I please tag along? "

Fin smiled, and the firefly laughed.

"The more the merrier," Fin said softly.

The night was full of laughter and songs.

When the morning came, the three

continued with their firefly search.

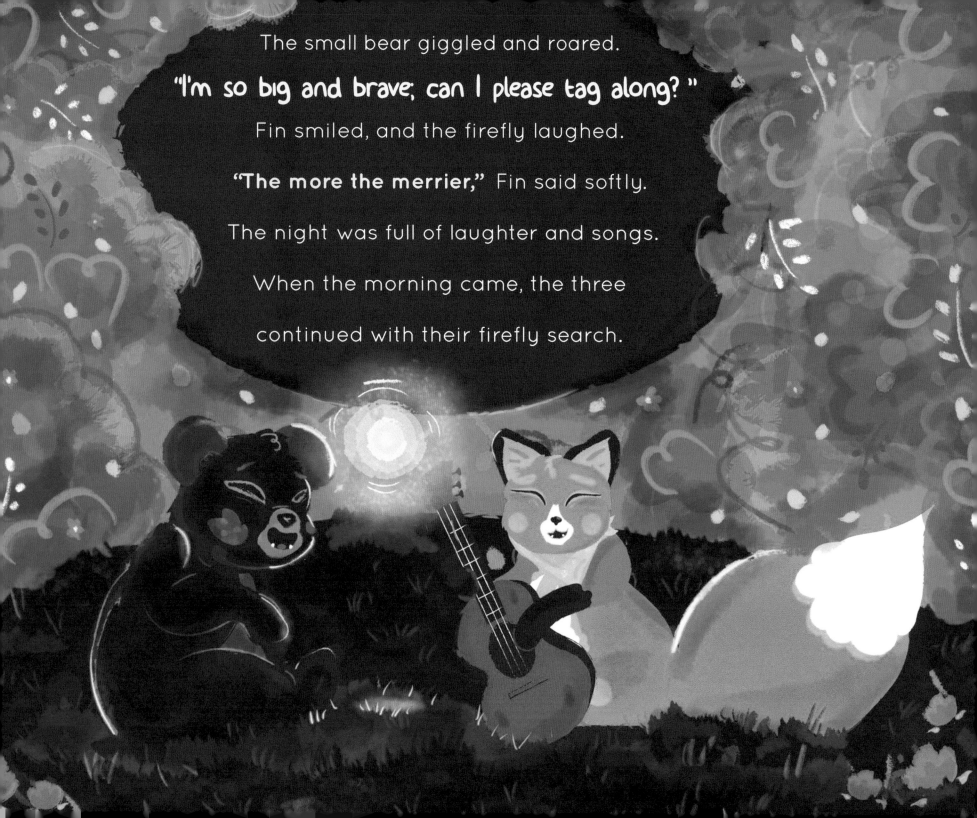

Deep between the trees they heard what sounded like thunder.

They found a giant cloud in a deep slumber.

His loud snores began to shake every nearby tree.

Inside of his belly, the fireflies were glowing,

shimmering, and fluttering about.

"Maybe we should wake him," gasped Fin.

"Great idea," said the bear, trembling. **"Go on ahead!"**

Fin stood in front of the cloud.

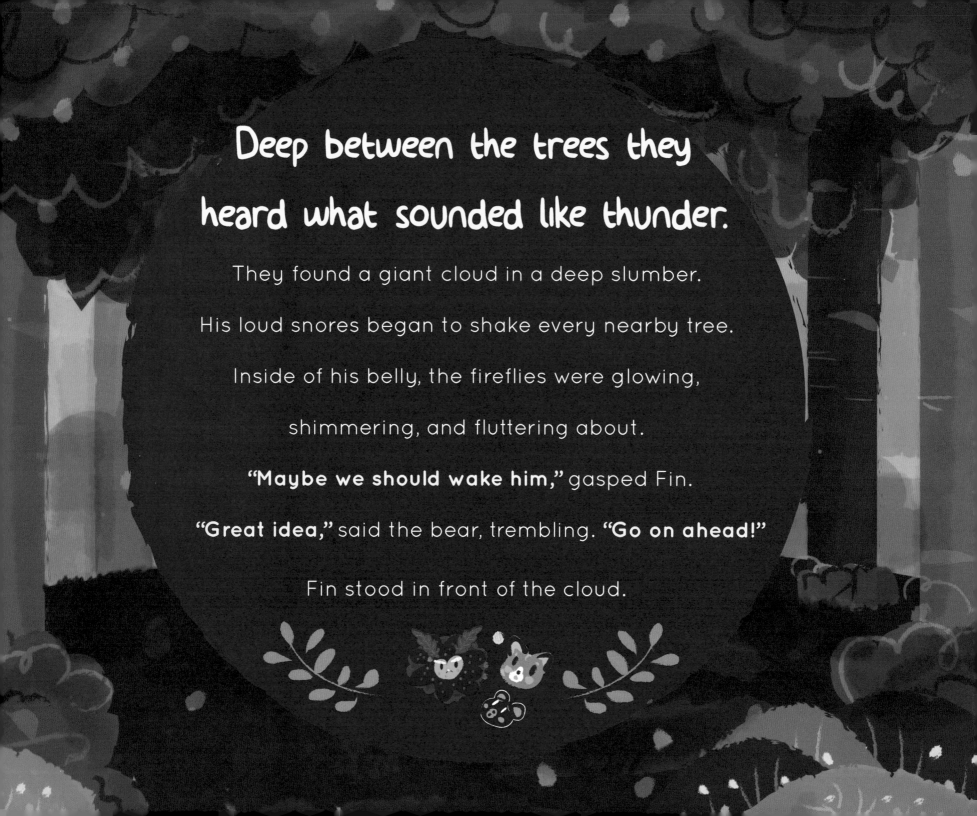

"Excuse me?
Can you please give
us our fireflies back?
You seem to have
ate them all but one. "

Fin tried his very best to be polite.

The cloud woke up with a loud snort!

He peered down at Fin, a very small fox.

"I have traveled a great distance, and I am in need of a good rest." he growled. "I am very tired, and you are one rude little fox."

Then the cloud huffed and puffed large gusts of wind toward Finn and his friends.

The gusts of wind were so strong!

The ground began to rumble,

and the stars shook above.

Fin held on tightly to the ground.

He did not want to be carried away!

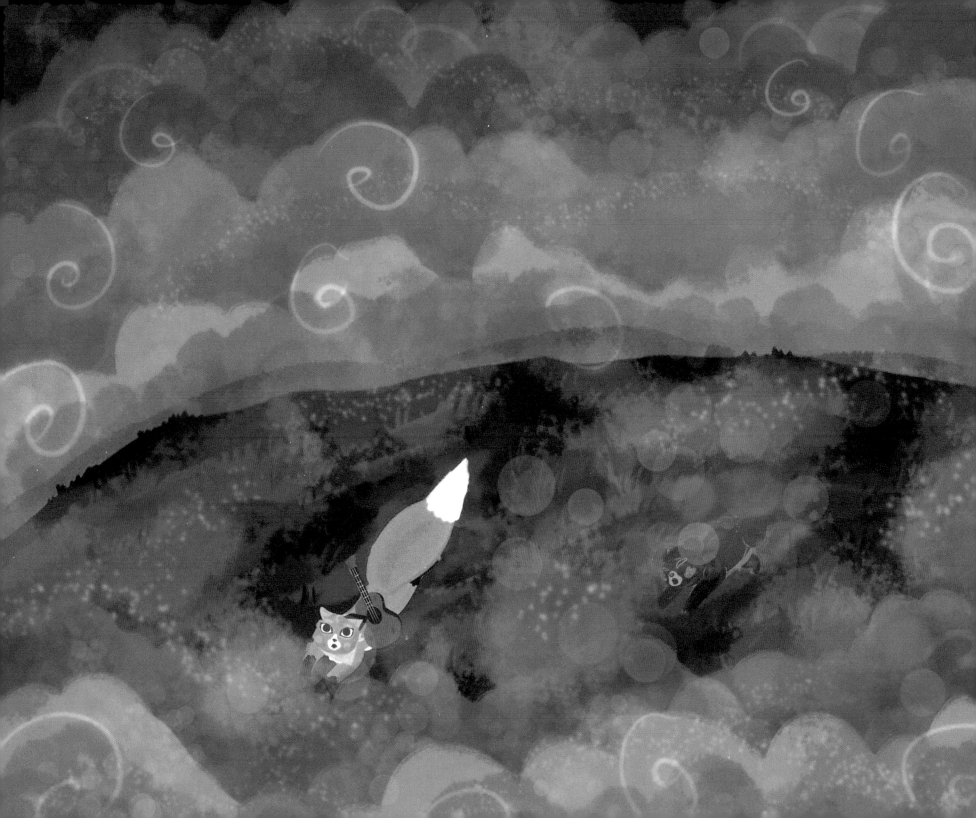

"I can't hold on
for much longer! "

the firefly called over to Fin.

The winds began to blow her away.

Fin knew that he had to do something!

"What could I possibly do?" thought Fin.

Fin held on tightly to his cherry wood guitar.

He thought about the fireflies and his new friends.

He thought about the songs they had sang together,

and the joy that it had brought to all of them.

Suddenly, Fin knew what to do.

Fin took a deep breath and strummed his guitar.

He played a happy melody that was heard near and far.

The most joyful music began to fill the air.

The young bear grabbed two sticks and tapped and

danced to the rhythm. The firefly sang the most beautiful song.

The fireflies inside of the cloud began to dance with glee.

They began to light WayWayYonder!

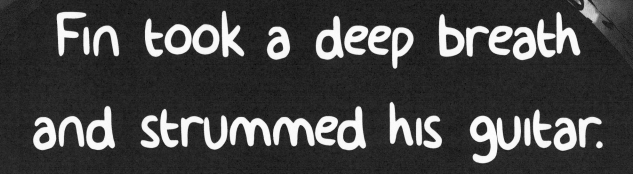

Deep in the woods of
WayWayYonder,

The animals rejoiced and the fireflies shimmered.

The large cloud watched the forest come to life.

"I am very sorry," he said sadly.

Fin felt sorry for the cloud. **"Well, if you promise to be more careful, maybe we can be friends?"** Fin smiled.

The cloud smiled back.

"I would like that very much."

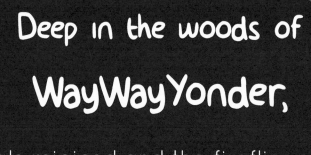

"Three cheers for Fin, the kind little fox!"

The bear and the firefly cheered on. Fin was happy. He had saved his home of **Way Way Yonder**, and gained three special friends. Fin looked around and thought how

his home had never looked so beautiful!

GREYSCALE

BIN TRAVELER FORM

Cut By _Dina_ Qty _63_ Date _5-30_

Scanned By _____ Qty _____ Date _____

Scanned Batch IDs _____

Notes / Exception _____